Without a Net

"Obra editada en el marco del Programa 'Sur' de Apoyo a las Traducciones del Ministerio de Relaciones Exteriores, Comercio Internacional y Culto de la República Argentina."

"Work published within the framework of 'Sur' Translation Support Program of the Ministry of Foreign Affairs, International Trade and Worship of the Argentine Republic."

Without a Net

Ana María Shua

Translations from the Spanish by Steven J. Stewart

Hanging Loose Press
Brooklyn, New York

Published by Hanging Loose Press, 231 Wyckoff Street, Brooklyn, New York, 11217. All Rights Reserved. No part of this book may be reproduced without the publisher's written permission, except for brief quotations in reviews.

www.hangingloosepress.com
Printed in the United States of America
10 9 8 7 6 5 4 3 2 1

Hanging Loose Press thanks the Literature Program of the New York State Council on the Arts for a grant in support of the publication of this book.

Cover art by Arnold Mesches: *The Greatest Show on Earth 6,* from the series *It's a Circus*. Acrylic on canvas.

Cover design by Marie Carter

Some of these pieces first appeared in *Global Grafitti* and *Hanging Loose*.

Library of Congress Cataloging-in-Publication Data available on request.

ISBN: 978-1-934909-28-7

Translator's Note

Though she has published over 80 books in a multitude of genres and has won numerous national and international awards, Ana María Shua is perhaps best known for being the "Queen of the Microstory" in the Spanish-speaking world on both sides of the Atlantic.

Microfictions are normally classified as short narrative pieces less than half a page long. Argentina is particularly notable for the genre, with such 20th-century masters as Borges, Cortázar, and Denevi standing out. Shua writes in the tradition of these authors by warping language and our sense of reality. Microfictions and the concision they embody are an increasingly apt literary form for our fast-paced, fragmented, and rapidly changing world.

This book is a collection of microfictions based on and revolving around the circus. The pieces here explore such themes as the absurdity of existence, the weight of expectations imposed on us by our roles in life, and the problematic nature of memory. In an interview in Spain's *El Mundo*, Shua describes her circus microfictions as "brief, phantasmagoric texts, translucent, something you can't look at head on. They demand that you concentrate and be distracted at the same time." Ernesto Calabuig has written that Shua's circus stories are "brilliant and elaborate, an ingenious variation on circus characters and tropes." And a review of Shua's book *Fenómenos de circo* (from which most of these pieces are drawn) in Spain's *El Público* observes that "joy, brilliance, and glitz mix in these brief texts that are performed with pirouettes of language, with the melancholy and sadness and nostalgia they share with the circus."

With my translations here, I have tried to stay faithful to the texts' original meanings, rhythms, and images while creating new texts that have a density and texture comparable to the originals.

While all translations are new, unique texts, I want mine to be works that the author herself can recognize as and be proud to call her own.

Many of the events and individuals mentioned in the book are real.

—Steven J. Stewart (15 March 2012; Rexburg, ID)

Contents: 99 Microfictions

Freaks

The Animals

Circus History

Prologue

Secret Wish

Deep in the heart of every child, every mother, every spectator, lies that secret wish to see the trapeze artist fall, to see him smash his bones against the ground, spill his dark blood on the sand, that fundamental wish to see the lions fight over the tamer's remains, the wish to see the horse drag the rider around with her foot caught in the stirrup, striking her head in rhythm against the edge of the ring, and for them we have launched this circus, the best, the ultimate, the circus where human pyramids collapse at their base, the knife thrower sinks his blades (by accident, always by accident) into his assistant's breast, the bear shreds the gypsy's face with his paw, and because of that, because the worst-case scenarios play out and because we always want what we don't have, the audience's desires shift: sick of disasters and failures they begin to wish that the trapeze artist's hands reach it in time, that the tamer keep the lions under control, that the rider make it back to the saddle, and instead of being filled with death and horror, the secret places of their hearts begin to brim with horrified kindness, with hope for the happiness of others, and thus they leave our show at peace with themselves, proud of their humanity, feeling they are better for it, that they are decent, sensitive, and well-intentioned people, the generous audience of the most perfect of circuses.

It's All a Circus

Dubious Circus

You believe you're at the circus, but you have doubts, you look for proof. The bear has your mother's face, and the word "acrobat," though it's pure sound, is made of red letters and is edible. Though you're not a woman, you're nursing a small tiger which is in no way a baby. You do everything you can to wake up with the sound of the orchestra, but the music is hypnotic, suffocating. With hands stiff from sleep, you manage to move the pillow off your nose and now can breathe better. None of this proves that you're not really at the circus. To make sure, you'll have to wake up, look around, verify that you haven't landed in another dream. And still.

The Ghost Circus

It turns up all at once. The carpenter's daughter notices that they never asked for sawdust or wood shavings like ordinary circuses. Everything is ready for the show to start. You don't see them set up the big top or take the animals out of their cages. The wagons are already empty, the performers already waiting their turn to enter the ring. The whole audience is translucent, except you, of course. Even the clowns carry chains. Children fear the ghost circus, adults pity it.

My Dream Circus

for Silvio

There are no drunken clowns nor horseback riders, there's no animal tamer nor submissive tiger, no gypsy making a bear dance ballet, no knife thrower or death-defying assistant, no acrobats, no trapeze artists, no candy venders, no jugglers, there are no dwarves, no big top, no banners, no gentle elephants, no magician with lightning fingers. Just you and I are there. And they clap for us.

The Poor Circus

In a poor circus each artist has to fill diverse roles. If we pay close attention, without being fooled by the changing outfits and makeup, we'll see them take advantage of their skills in distinctive ways. For example, the tightrope walker is the horseback rider, the acrobats are contortionists, the circus boss is the ticket keeper and also the magician (with the public as well as the creditors). Some are more difficult to discover, because they choose very dissimilar roles, like the trapeze artist who is also the trained monkey (or the other way around), the elephants who work as ushers, the clowns who transform into rings of fire. But the most difficult role is that of the tamer—who is also the tiger—when he has to place his head inside his own mouth.

The Poorest Circus

The Papelito circus still goes through small towns all over Argentina, modest and picturesque. Its first big top was made from burlap bags and the spectators had to bring their own seats.

But there was another circus that was even poorer. Besides bringing their own seats, the spectators had to sit down and pretend they were watching the ring, to imagine it.

The Evolution of the Circus

The ancient Romans thought it was appropriate to watch lions attack, kill, and devour human beings. In bullfights, the animal has fewer options, though it has the opportunity to defend itself and is sometimes spared. In the circuses of my childhood, the tamed animals did what the tamer commanded: it was a show of pure obedience, a quality that humans tend to confuse with intelligence, as if rebelliousness were anything but the most obvious sign of thinking for oneself. But in today's circus there are no animals; our presence is considered neither proper nor instructive; much is made of the punishments and tortures we endure when being trained. Like the armless man and the bearded woman, we tamed animals have fallen out of favor. What good, for example, is a she-bear who is a gifted writer in such an illiterate world? I for one hope they start feeding us people again.

Logical Fallacies

You don't always get to the truth through logical reasoning. It would be logical to suppose, for example, that natives of other planets would choose the circus as their natural refuge. It would be logical to suppose they would feel protected by the thick layers of a clown's makeup, that they would choose to exhibit their differences from human beings instead of hiding them, that they would show off and not hide their exotic skills with the trapeze, that they would be interested in the nomadic life of the circus.

In reality, they prefer to blend in with the inhabitants of big cities, to not call attention to themselves. The nomadic life forces you to live in close quarters with very few people for long periods of time. It's true that some work in the circus, but only as temporary laborers.

Introduction to the Circus

I toss a rounded noun into the air. With a singular, well-aimed shot, before it falls, I perforate its very center with an adjective. I juggle verbs, I walk along the slack wire of risky syntax. In the midst of extreme contortions, I whip the words and make them leap through the rings of fire of unexpected meaning. Then, in all its variety and splendor, in lush and glitzy detail, the circus emerges. You are the audience, the show is for you alone; please, applaud the wild animals and don't say anything to the people waiting outside.

Watching the Circus

Lying in bed, he watches the circus on television. The screen is large, the view is perfect, it's the best circus in the world. A man flies while attached to an elastic cord that allows him to soar through the air. If I'd started when I was a kid, thinks the viewer, if I'd spent a lot of time practicing .... His muscles tense up under his pajamas. He doesn't even want the applause but rather the sensation of flying, to have absolute control over every inch of this body that's growing soft, getting old and decaying on the mattress, with no hope, no destiny.

Circus Music

He's chosen circus music for his cell phone's ring tone: it's a sound that's vital, imperious, full of magic and gems, and it wouldn't surprise him at all if it summoned elephants, dwarves, wagons, wild animals, tightrope walkers, and monkeys, it wouldn't surprise him if they materialized right here, in the bank lobby where the teller waits on him with awkward courtesy, where a policeman approaches him to kindly ask him to shut off his phone for security reasons, it wouldn't surprise him but it doesn't happen, the music doesn't summon anything—on the contrary, with each call it takes him a little farther away from the circus, from his childhood.

Why?

Why insist on jumping from one stool to another, why singe ourselves jumping through the fiery hoops, why walk in a straight line shaking out our hair, why walk upright, why do somersaults or dance on two legs when the cage has disappeared, when no one is whipping us, when it's been years since we've seen or heard from the tamer?

Pepino the Clown

A friend is waiting for me in a café. As I arrive, I see her profile like an ancient coin—her stark, beautiful outline. She tells me about a famous clown from her childhood, perhaps he was English, his name might have been Pepino. But Pepino doesn't exist anymore, nor does her childhood, nor does mine. The circus, which we used to look forward to with gleeful anticipation, now surrounds us, invades us, creeps in through the gaps. There's a circus all around us and we just want it to go away. To put it out of sight, we drink our coffee.

Perseus and the Head of Medusa

Perseus is good. I like it, it has a nice sound. We could call you "Perseus the Great." And what do you need for your act? We've got great lighting and a knockout sound system. The Helm of Hades to make yourself invisible? Sorry, look, you'd have to supply that sort of thing yourself—it would be part of your act. Yes, the same with the flying sandals. I get it: They were loaned to you and you had to give them back to Hermes. But you've got a lot of stage presence. I think you could make it work no matter what you had. Take, for example, that bag you've got right there. Oh, I get it. No, you don't have to show me. Medusa's head is dangerous. Couldn't you water down her gaze a little? Maybe some thick contact lenses? We could use a mirror to put them on her. That way the audience would feel something strange, but it wouldn't completely turn them . . . . Though deep down . . . . I'd say you try it at one of the shows and see what happens, we won't have any problems. Believe me, Perseus my friend, deep down, the audience is already made of stone.

Circus Prometheus

Art or entertainment? If the vulture digs his beak deep into Prometheus's liver, is it art or entertainment?

It's art if it's blood dyeing the bird's beak, if it's blood spouting and gushing from the body, if it's blood reddening the rocks the man is chained to. But if it's a mixture of glycerin and ketchup, it's just entertainment, a big circus. Of course, there are those who believe it's the other way around.

Meanwhile, since we can't check it from this far away, you just have to enjoy the spectacle. There's a show every day.

Math Class

What's going on, I shout angrily, seeing my students greet me with pirouettes and clowning around. Take out a sheet of paper for a pop quiz on logarithms. Anger turns my voice into a roar. People have begun to gather outside, other students, other teachers, who peer in through the classroom windows and enthusiastically applaud. A math class is not a circus, I roar again but, when one of my students cracks his whip and forces me to climb up on the platform, I start to doubt, I'm no longer sure.

The Automatons

They are men, women, and children who excel in the art of imitating life. They are so perfect in mimicking human movements that only their constant repetition betrays the fact that they are wooden dummies. Their owner and creator is outstanding in his attention to detail, such as the shine on their skin, the dimensions of their flesh. One of the men has a tic; one of the women, her eyes empty, wears a half smile, as if she's remembering something; a child with a cold sniffles.

But if they are almost perfect in imitating life, you should see their absolute perfection in dying, the gradual paleness that takes hold of their cheeks, the unresponsive abandonment of their bodies, the surprising, surprising speed with which the wood rots.

The Performers

Immortal

Tired of sewing on sequins, I decided that being an artist was just a question of time and discipline. I decided that immortality was all I would need to be a trapeze artist, acrobat, or animal tamer, to shine beneath the big top's lights in a sequined dress that had been sewn by someone else.

Two hundred years later I'm still a costume designer. A talented but slightly old-fashioned costume designer. I'm mostly sought after when the ebb and flow of fashion brings us back to epochs I know better than anyone. And yet, at night, when the show is over and I'm drinking beer with my new, always new, friends, I don't want to die. Sequins are no longer hand-sewn, the beer is cold and bitter; I like it, like before, when it comes without much fizz.

Trapeze Artists

Don't be afraid: She'll fly, she inherited our genes, says the trapeze artist. And from the heights, he launches his daughter, still a baby, through the air, toward the arms of his terrified, unfaithful wife. Don't be afraid: Through the arts of her true father, the magician, the girl really does fly. Or makes them believe she's flying.

Flyers and Catchers

In every acrobatic act there are flyers and catchers. The catchers lift and sustain, the flyers do flips. The catchers propel, the flyers soar through the air. The catchers form the bases of pyramids, the flyers balance and hold poses high in the air. The catcher catches, the flyer is caught. At this moment, I am the catcher, and you are the flyer. This is the only circus that allows us to switch roles.

Angel in the Ring

No, there's nothing interesting about watching him fly, because he does after all have wings. It's like watching a man walk, like watching a fish swim. Now if this angel of yours could do a trick that went against his nature, against his anatomy. Could he throw knives, for example? Now we're getting there. What did you say his name was? Azrael, Azrael—that sounds familiar. But here we'd have to give him a stage name, something stronger, more artistic, easier to pronounce. We could call him, say, "The Angel of Death." That would get the audience going. Ah, I get it. That's his specialty. No, he doesn't have to show me. But, you know, that's a pretty common trick. Even a kid . . . What if we had him do the opposite? That would be impressive! Oh. I see. It's not his thing. Look, leave him with me a few days, no commitment, and we'll find something we can do with him, especially if he's discreet. You know, everybody's got enemies. And creditors.

The Acrobats

Just like porn stars or ice skaters, acrobats are always repeating the same moves in different combinations. Looking desperately for something original, the acrobats' union holds a contest to award a prize for a truly new act.

Most of the competitors offer small variations of existing acts, changing up the height of the leaps or the number of acrobats involved. For example, one group of 5,400 men and women leap together in a synchronized and coordinated way. It's a nice show, without a doubt, the judges opine, but not so much original as expensive.

The winner is a lean Hungarian artist with thin blond hair who surprises everyone by somersaulting out of reality. It's too bad he can't come back to claim his prize.

Bellerophon and Chimera

Once every show, sometimes twice a day, Bellerophon, mounted on Pegasus, kills Chimera.

Bellerophon is attractive and wears clothes that show off his Greek-hero musculature. The hind part of Chimera's body is a snake's tail, she has the torso and front legs of a lion, and she has an odd-looking goat's head that spits out flames.

Bellerophon places a piece of lead on his lance point. The flames coming from Chimera's mouth melt the lead, which turns to liquid in her mouth and kills her.

The fight, of course, is an act. Exiled from their place and time, Bellerophon and Chimera share a lot of memories. Over and over the beast pretends to die to the applause of the stupid audience members, who also fail to believe that Pegasus can fly in spite of seeing him with their own eyes.

Sword Swallowers' Misfortunes

Sword swallowers are seldom talked about. They're cursed by the fact that the audience can only see part of their act. For this reason, half of their act is designed to demonstrate that the other half isn't a trick. Many have died trying to prove something.

Signor Benedetti would swallow objects given to him by the audience. According to a Havana newspaper in 1874, at one event he swallowed a general's sword and several canes but failed in an attempt to swallow an umbrella.

Maud Churchill would pass her sword among the crowd so that people could examine it. In 1926, performing before the King and Queen of England, a spectator nicked the blade. Maud died several days later, believing that she had finally proven the authenticity of her act.

In 1947, Tony Marino was the first to swallow a neon tube and light it to demonstrate that it wasn't a trick. The circus erupted in applause. The artist, caught up in the moment, bowed. They saved him in a hospital in Detroit.

In a town in Hungary in 1952, the German artist Stephan Baum swallowed a skeptical spectator whole. When a microphone was near his esophagus, a voice could clearly be heard saying "Turn on the light. This is a trick."

The Disguise

In the circus, when he's disguised as a clown, his clumsiness is hardly noticeable. The white makeup covers his paleness. His co-workers sometimes complain that he smells bad, but the circus owner defends him because he gets more laughs than anyone, he doesn't ask for much, and almost nobody realizes he's dead.

A Marvel of Flying Poetry

When Alfredo Codona, a Mexican trapeze artist, first achieved the triple somersault in 1920, the newspapers called him a "marvel of flying poetry" and an "angel of the trapeze." Codona was shocked. He always worked with a safety net, to perfect his disguise, and he was sure that he had been flawless in concealing his wings.

The Great Garabagne

Magic has its limits. Not even the boldest magician dares to promise to be able to grant every wish, not even every simple wish, of his audience members. But the Great Garabagne promises, with a great display of artifice, the opposite. With his magic he can make it so that your wishes never come true. His fame around the world keeps growing as no one dares put him to the test.

Icarians and Antipodists

In the bas-reliefs of Ancient Egypt there appear women performing Icarian feats. Icarians, like antipodists, juggle with their feet. While antipodists use objects, Icarians use children. Do-gooders complain that the children are put in danger. But they're treated with great care: A well-trained child is hard to replace.

On one occasion, a child who had been propelled high in the air by his father's feet refused to come down, and he was adopted by a family of high-wire walkers. The child lived from then on in the heights and got used to sleeping on the slack wire without even letting go of his pole. When the circus was disassembled and transported to another town, the high-wire walkers would tie a short rope for him across the bed of the truck. In his later years he became a good friend of the protagonist of Calvino's *The Baron in the Trees*, though—perhaps because he was a commoner—he's never mentioned in the book.

Illusionists and Witches

Before the 20th century, illusionists were required to reveal their tricks to the authorities to avoid being prosecuted for witchcraft. Many true witches had to pretend to be illusionists to survive. For their part, to enter into the closed and secret world of the true witches, many illusionists had to pretend to be witches pretending to be illusionists. But the true witches always found them out.

Questions

In his *History of the Circus*, Dominique Mauclair claims to have witnessed in India an act that was described in the 19th century by a journalist from Paris, which is today practiced on the streets of Japan and has even been performed on American television. It's a regurgitation act that we might call "the human fountain."

According to Mauclair, with the help of some assistants, the artist drinks about 2 ½ gallons of water. To make the act more colorful, he also swallows several little red fish, some frogs, and a small snake. The spectators choose which they want to see regurgitated. The artist goes along, expelling the fish, frogs, and snake.

This man, when he's thirsty, what does he drink? What does he dream about? Does he have a laptop or want one? The fish, do they die with each performance, or do they survive? Does he earn enough to send his kids to school? Does he know when he's going to die, or does he imagine it? The frogs, are they trained? How does he do it in order? Does he fall in love? Is he happier than you are? Does he change the snake often?

The Gypsy

She doesn't guess the future. She sees it, she really sees it, in images like holograms, in her crystal ball. They are always useless snippets of her clients' lives, pieces of the future that are irrelevant but very clear, very defined. She sees them washing their hands in a restroom at a café, sunbathing at an unrecognizable beach, scratching a foot, adding pepper to a bowl of soup. Experience has taught her to deduce certain useful facts from these banal images. If they look very old, they'll have a long life. The way they dress or act can let her foretell good fortune. But she knows she can also get things completely wrong. For example, she once saw her own husband driving a luxury automobile—right before he got a job at a valet parking garage. It's all the same in the end. In any case, with her clients she always lies.

Lord Mystery

Gifted like none other when it came to circus arts, the English aristocrat we'll call Lord Mystery was capable of doing a triple somersault on the trapeze, of keeping twelve plates spinning at once, of amazing the audience with his magic acts, of dominating eight lions and fifteen tigers locked together with him in a cage, of keeping two ashtrays and a book and four balls in the air at once, but he couldn't fall in love, perhaps because it wasn't a trick or an illusion, nor was it a matter of skill.

Magic

A male and female of the same species (including *homo sapiens*) join certain areas of their bodies, those that are most different. Inside the woman's womb, the masculine and feminine rudiments of each fuse together, and, from that union, a new being begins to form which will be born in a time frame that varies according to the species: almost two years in the case of elephants, nine months in the case of human beings, much less for insects. It requires patience because it's a slow act, but it's very impressive, especially for children. Many of the accompanying physical and chemical processes are known, but to this point no one has been able to discover the trick or copy it.

Magician and Saw

With his saw, the magician begins cutting the box from which extend the legs, arms, and head of his assistant. The woman's face, smiling at first, is replaced by a mask of fear. She promptly begins screaming. Blood spurts, the woman howls, begging for help, thrashing her arms and legs with apparent desperation while the audience applauds and laughs. Afterwards she makes some feeble cries and eventually grows quiet. In the past the audience was more demanding, the magician remembers: they wanted to see the woman reappear intact. Now everything is easier. Except, of course, finding assistants.

Magician Without a Script

Once, many years ago (too many, now), a young magician asked me to write a script for his show. I asked him to prepare a list of the tricks he could do, to link them together along the narrative thread of a small story. I found his response unexpected and hardly professional. I'm a magician, he said. I can do anything.

I didn't believe him, and I regret it. How much less chaotic this would all be if he'd had a good script!

Many Versions

Trying to escape, the hamster runs on the desperate wheel that forms part of its prison. Perhaps the cruelest thing is the torment of hope. Nevertheless, a child absorbed in watching sees only a miniature circus show where the hamster is an acrobat running for the pleasure of running, for the applause.

In the real circus, the acrobat, the magician, the tightrope walker—are they trying to escape as well? It's said that a certain trapeze artist managed it once, that he was able to get away for good. It's also said he came back of his own free will. Others say he wanted to come back but couldn't. Others say he was brought back by force. Some even suppose that we're all free.

Gordian Knot

Gordias, king of Phrygia, had an ox cart that was tied with a knot so complicated that no one could untie it. According to the oracle, whoever was capable of undoing the knot could conquer all of Asia Minor. Only Alexander the Great was capable of finding the solution: he cut the knot with a stroke of his sword.

But this is different, guys, please, just have a little more patience, insists the young contortionist to the men who carried him off the platform and have been trying to unknot her for the past three days.

The Perfect Clown

There's nothing more hilarious than someone else's failures. Clowns fail spectacularly in all their undertakings and the audience laughs and laughs. The perfect clown fails even in his attempts to entertain the spectators, who get bored or just sad looking at him. It's the absolute culmination of his art, but few understand it. Fired from the circus, no one wants to hire him and he walks the streets dejectedly, less funny than ever, followed by a group of graduate students who consider him a cult figure. With time, he'll earn a living giving seminars. His country nominates him for the Grock Prize, the Nobel for clowns.

Who's the Patsy?

Clowns work in pairs. Normally one of them is the victim of the jokes, tricks, and schemes of the other; one of them gets slapped around. The pairs might be Pierrot and Harlequin, Augusto and Carablanca, the *penasar* and the *kartala*, the stupid one and the smart one, the fat one and the thin one, the clumsy one and the agile one, the author and the reader.

The Shooter

In the small circuses out West, there was a famous shooter who would display his art. To become a crack shot requires aptitude, vocation, and tireless practice. Our man had worked at developing his marksmanship to the point of being able to put a bullet through a dime at fifty paces. A few hours before dying he explained his miserable downfall to one Dr. Pemberton: None of the outlaws attacking him were carrying change.

The Snake Swallower

" It took three months to learn how to swallow swords and snakes. At first I hurt my swallow with the swords. During the first two months I couldn't eat solid foods. I cured myself with sugar and lemon. My snakes are eighteen inches long and have a roughish, queer taste. For half a penny the kids bring them to me from the forest. They're dirty; before swallowing them I scrape them off with a rag and pull out their stingers.

Swallowing snakes is easy. They go down soft, even though their scales are a little rough coming out. I put their heads in my mouth and hold their tails tight with my nails. Trying to get away, the snake thrusts its head into my throat and the rest of its front curls into my mouth. It's really a trick—the snake's head doesn't go more than two inches down my swallow."

London, 1860. So confesses the great Sallementro, almost embarrassed. And you, what would you be willing to do for some applause?

Swallowing Poison

Captain Veitro's show consisted of swallowing poisons. He was honest, dedicated to his profession, and like many others wanted to prove it. By killing a chick, a dove, or a rabbit, he demonstrated the potency of the poison he was ready to ingest. After swallowing it, he would vomit it up to prove it had really been inside his stomach. His act was not especially successful. Even the public has limits, sometimes.

Ventriloquist and Dummy

Like another self, cheeky and rebellious, without the limits imposed by good manners, the ventriloquist's dummy says what his owner never would. That's his job. Sometimes he goes too far; some spectators get offended and the ventriloquist is forced to chide him in a polite and moderated way. The dummy is also a writer, but his owner erases or destroys all his work.

The Maze of Terror

Some years ago there was a newspaper ad asking for people with great bodily or facial defects or who were extremely ugly. Someone had come up with a new terror attraction for an amusement park: Visitors would have to pass through a shadowy maze where monstrous beings with fake hatchets would chase after them. There's nothing more terrifying than monsters who are real people, without makeup, authentically horrible. Thus they hired men and women who had been mutilated by accidents, serious burns, or birth defects. Following the general trend of society, they tried to replace representation with reality: Roman circus instead of Greek theater.

Attracted by the ad, many freaks left the circus for the amusement park. And everything worked out well until a couple of adolescent girls complained of having been trapped and groped by the employees in charge of scaring them.

The monsters assured their defense attorney that in reality they themselves were the mistreated girls, to whom, through contact, the true monsters had transmitted their horror, freeing themselves of it. The lawyer advised them to drop that story, which obviously no one would believe.

The new attraction, considered a dangerous failure, was shut down forever. After serving a light sentence, the freaks returned to (or joined for the first time) the circus.

Famous Fighters

The Chilean Joaquín Maluenda Liberona, also known as "The Savage Clown," was a circus strongman. For his act he fought against a bull. To prove that the fight was authentic, it was a different bull every time, and he'd get it from whichever town the circus was visiting.

In Argentina, the clown Pastichoti fought against a muzzled bear whose claws had been removed. While the man rained down wild punches against its body and snout, the bear squeezed his head between its front paws until blood started flowing from his eyes and ears.

Nothing compares, however, to the fight between a man and his griefs, regrets, and addictions: a bloody spectacle, not for children's eyes. Come and see.

Family Fights

Family fights are rare in our circus, even at New Year's parties. Offense is usually involuntary and quickly forgotten. Think about it: you're not going to pick a fight with your brother-in-law the knife thrower. Or get on the bad side of your father-in-law the lion tamer. Even the tightrope walker and horseback rider are all muscle. And it's not even a good idea to bother the dwarves: there's a lot of them and they stick together. Because of all this, whenever there's the hint of a fight, the magician is called in to make it disappear. It might be that his magic is just an illusion, but he's great at keeping the peace.

The Animal Tamer

"Behold!" demands the tamer.

And the circus director beholds, a little bored.

"Jump!" shouts the tamer. His orders are immediately obeyed. "Jump, jump!" he shouts again.

There are flaming hoops, high and long leaps, acrobatic tricks and processions. The show is traditional but also has a distinctive flair.

The circus director doesn't want to disparage any artist. He applauds enthusiastically so as not to discourage the tamer.

"An excellent show," he assures him. "But it's not for us. You see, with our audiences, skill isn't enough. You need a sense of danger. Your vegetables are well trained, but they're not threatening enough. Perhaps you could try the same thing with carnivorous plants . . . ."

The tamer, sad and angry, gives the order to attack, and even though he immediately regrets it and tries to stop things it's too late, the circus director lies at his feet, needlessly murdered. This is the weak point of my act, the man thinks, as he escapes. And it's true: Once the fury of the pumpkins is unleashed it's always hard for him to control them.

Pies in the Face

Pies in the face, always pies in the face, why not puddings on the feet, pastries in the stomach, noodles with white sauce on the shoulder blades . . . Tired of the monotonous routine of the circus, the clown gets a job at the complaints department of a large store, where he's still the one always getting slapped around, but at least now no one's laughing at him.

The Triple Somersault

Somersaults are dangerous, truly dangerous. To achieve them, the thrill-seeking trapeze artist uses a faux safety wire, a net that—he knows perfectly well—couldn't hold his weight. Like an addict, he needs his fix: The thrill-seeking trapeze artist needs to feel the immanence of death. With a triple somersault, the sensation is so intense that his entire life passes before his eyes. Because of this, as he gets older, he needs to prolong the leap, to give his memory more time. At eighty years old, a master of his art, he crosses the ocean from one continent to another in a triple somersault that lets him examine his whole life in detail.

The Business

Everybody thinks about the performers, about those irresponsible tumblers, all of them easily replaceable, nobody thinks about the financial problems, about the complexity of a business with so many contracts involved. The circus is no longer just about the ticket—there are television rights, Internet sites . . . And the taxes! Trust me, a good bookkeeper is a magician (the opposite rarely being the case).

Advantages to Being Women

Who if not women, always willing to bend (men are so straight),
with our complicated and convoluted style (men are so simple),
with our loose joints (men's are so rigid), who if not women and
snakes to act as contortionists, tied in that knot that's so obscene,
so tempting, so reprehensible, so in demand, so praised.

The Sphere of Death

For the motorcycle riders of the Sphere of Death, launching themselves at high speeds in all directions inside that ball made of crisscrossing iron bars is nothing more than an everyday routine. What do they do then when they want to experience fear or danger? Eat fruit without washing it? Have unprotected sex? Insult the strongman's mother? Annoy the elephants? Do they go to the dentist? Sleep with the lion tamer's wife? Do they get married?

Freaks

Diane Arbus

With morbid childlike curiosity and thrilling subtlety, the photographer Diane Arbus (1923-1971) chose to capture the tragic beauty of monsters. She became an artist in the same field that Barnum grew in as a promoter. Arbus became a famous, feared, and finally sought-after freak hunter. It's said that two girls were sewn together solely to appear in one of her pictures. It's said that an adult male consented to have his head transplanted onto a fat child's body for the same reason. Her suicide—as with every corpse—transformed her into one of them.

Send in the Artist

Okay, so your artist is missing his feet, but that's not enough. What can he do? At least walk on his hands? That's a pretty common skill, but with a footless man we could get something out of it. I see. He doesn't have hands either. It would be great if he could do some sort of acrobatic act with his stumps.

No arms or legs? Okay, now we're talking. A snake man. Did you ever see Prince Randian in that movie *Freaks*?

Hmm. So, if I understand you right, his torso . . . .

And his head? A talking head always makes an impression, especially if we can show that it's not a trick. Not even that? This is getting better by the minute. Why don't you bring him by so I can see him? Ah, now I get it. He's already here.

Barnum's Agents

P.T. Barnum's agents traveled the whole world looking for freaks who were ever more distinctive, stranger, more terrifying. It was important, however, that they maintained something of their human form, because only a deformation of the normal and familiar can provoke that effect of horror and fascination. Thus the agents were forced to reject some very interesting specimens, like the man-book of Kinuria, whom people could read from the first page to the last without imagining for an instant that he had been born of woman.

The Man with the Power

When his parents realized he had the Power, they imagined a future for him filled with glory. Nevertheless, success doesn't depend on ability, no matter how magical it may be, but rather on the right combination of smarts and willpower. Someone else might have become king of the world. This man hardly manages to make a living as a circus freak.

Still, the traveling life suits him. Hundreds of children attend every show. From the ring he has a panoramic view of the audience and can thus detect *Them*. They are few, they are rare. He recognizes them every time by their evasive gestures, by their sad looks. They are the ones with the Power. After the show, he stands at the exit and pats the children's heads. It's only on the few that he bestows a poison that causes a painless, almost harmless death the next day. "My suffering," he tells himself to justify this, "is worse."

The Ambassadors from Mars

The brothers George and Willie Muse were kidnapped by unscrupulous promoters. They were first exhibited as Iko and Eko, the Ecuadorian Cannibals, and some years later as the Ambassadors from Mars.

In reality, only one of them, Willie, was a Martian, but he never achieved the rank of ambassador. He was sent to earth and implanted into his supposed mother's womb at the same instant George was conceived. The original plan was that he would develop and be born as the twin brother of a normal child.

Unfortunately for the planned invasion, the other occupant of this particular uterus turned out to be a very rare combination of genes: a black albino. The twins were so strange that they soon became circus attractions and the Martian operatives, not wanting attention, abandoned the experiment. Willie Muse died on Earth, at 108 years of age, 30 years after his twin brother.

Tiny Lucia Zarate

As an adult, the Mexican Lucia Zarate was 20 inches tall. She weighed five and a half pounds and was perfectly normal in every other way. She was the best-paid dwarf in history. In 1880, she earned no less than $20 an hour. She died one night of hypothermia when the train she was traveling on got stranded in the Sierra Nevada mountains.

Those who go on a pilgrimage to the site of her death consider her an intercessor before deity. Sitting at the feet of God's throne, she is the only one in the whole hierarchy of saints capable of resolving the small problems the others disdain. We plead with you, oh smallest Lucia, to save us from calluses, bad breath, untimely visitors, people who talk at the movies, food stains on clothing, and itchy allergic reactions.

The Human Skeleton

Pete Robinson, the Human Skeleton, weighed less than seventy pounds. He was notorious among other circus performers for how passionately he defended his political opinions. He was married to the fat woman Bunny Smith, a 460-pound beauty. Nevertheless, in Tod Browning's film *Freaks*, Pete played the husband of the bearded lady. Nothing can be so brutally obvious as reality.

Sacrifices for Love

Jean Carroll, a famous bearded woman, chose to shave off her beard to marry the contortionist John Carson. From her childhood, Jean had always been a circus attraction, and it wasn't easy for her to make a living any other way. So she decided to tattoo her body with 700 intricate decorative motifs that she successfully exhibited from that point on. It was a painful process, and I'm giving it as an example. Would you choose to eliminate those hideous extremities that you people call legs and arms to marry me? Our surgeons could replace them with the more pleasant appendages that are common to these parts. The rest of you is sufficiently strange in this world to keep on exhibiting without any problem.

It's All Relative

It's all relative. Here I'm a circus freak, says the sad female from Alpha Centauri, shaking out her vibrating appendages. On my planet, I won beauty contests; I was the equivalent of the Earth's Miss Universe. All in all, who can say she's lying?

The King of the Martian Pygmies

Phineas Taylor Barnum was the greatest promoter of circus freaks in the history of humanity. His agents scoured the whole world looking for deformities that were sufficiently terrifying to be exhibited for money. Not content with authentic horrors produced by nature, Barnum also displayed all types of fake freaks, living or embalmed, like the famous Feejee mermaid, a trick that caused hysteria among the inhabitants of New York. The Feejee mermaid didn't look like a woman. It was a phantasmagoric little creature with a pained expression, made from a simple deception: a stuffed salmon tail sewn onto the body of a monkey.

On the other hand, the tiny little man that the Barnum Museum used to exhibit in formalin with the pompous title of "King of the Martian Pygmies" was in reality an inhabitant of a planet that orbited our star, Epsilon Eridani. I recognized him immediately and stood there, with tears in my eyes, saying goodbye to my friend, while the indifferent crowd passed by.

Monster Fair

Though freak shows aren't prohibited, they're no longer considered an appropriate form of entertainment. At a neighborhood meeting, everyone agrees to allow the circus to set up, but to prohibit the monster fair that accompanies it.

One of the monsters stands on the platform to defend his work. "What else do you want us to do with all these poor human beings?" he painfully asks his indignant audience. And he doesn't say it out of self-pity, but because he knows the word "human" always moves the earthlings.

The Animals

Blacaman and Koringa

The Cuban miracle worker Blacaman, with the help of his assistant (and later competitor) Koringa, would hypnotize lions and crocodiles in the Mexican circus. His detractors insist the lions were drugged and the crocodiles were faking it for the money.

The Fake Horse

It looks like the old trick that's always a hit with kids: the fake horse. An upright man wearing an animal's head moves forward. Behind, covered by fabric that's made out to be the horse's body, goes a crouching man holding the other's waist. The fake horse goes around the ring a few times, does a few tricks, and afterwards the men separate to reveal the trick amid the applause. Thus we see the whole body of the man in back. On the other hand, we only ever see the legs of the man in front; who knows why he never takes off that happy, pleasant horse head made out of papier mâché? Most people assume he's also a clown.

Animal Rights

During the second half of the twentieth century, the growing concern for animal rights hit traditional circuses hard. In 1982, the tiny Fallon Circus in the United States was accused of starving and torturing its animals, which were exhibited in tiny, filthy cages and were mercilessly whipped at every event, to the audience's pleasure and outrage. The prosecutor dropped the charges when it was proven that in every case the victims were actors in disguise.

The Dragon

The problem is that the dragon doesn't know how to do anything. He's too old to fly and can hardly manage a pathetic liftoff like that of a chicken. Though two columns of smoke do weakly ascend from his scaly nostrils, he's no longer capable of expelling his punishing fire. He's interesting, the director says, very interesting, but better suited to a zoo than a circus. When the time comes, he could be stuffed and make a fine addition to any museum.

And the owner, or perhaps the dragon's agent, leaves the circus depressed, his troupe of winged species in tow: a sluggish-looking griffin, a family of vegetarian vampires, a former angel who clumsily displays the stumps of his amputated wings.

The Liger

The liger, according to the encyclopedias, is produced by mating a male lion with a female tiger. It looks like a gigantic lion with some diffuse tiger stripes. Male ligers have manes. Their scientific name is *Panthera tigris x panthera leo*.

Bigger than its mother and father, a liger can grow to more than 13 feet long and weigh up to 900 pounds. As the gene that limits growth is transmitted maternally in lions and paternally in tigers, the liger doesn't inherit it and thus never stops growing its whole life.

The tigon (also called tigron and tigral) is a cross between a male tiger and female lion: it's a smaller, more stylized animal, hardly imposing. That's why it's less common than the liger, the latter being an animal that's sought after, raised, and exploited by the circus, one that's never found in nature.

It's said that the biggest liger is bigger than anything we've ever seen. It's said that the whole universe, from the Big Bang on, is growing and expanding in the mouth of that most ancient liger, which is about to die.

The Spider Dance

No, I'm not interested in the spider dance, I'm sorry. Please, don't talk to me about how ancient the act is. From the Muromachi period, before the Edo period, you already said that. Yesterday somebody offered me a menhir-balancing act that was prehistoric, and I wasn't interested in that either. Look, it's an issue of infrastructure, this is a big top, we can't string interlocking nets between the beams like they do in Japanese temples. Besides, I'm not stupid, you know as well as I do what happened when the dance moved from being a religious rite to an acrobatic act, with the nets a long way from the ground. Exactly. There's a reason they stopped doing it, even in Japan. No, not even with a safety wire. But, wait a minute, don't hang up. What else do your spiders know how to do?

The Lions and the Tamer

Several lions agree to buy themselves a tamer, but they're poor. All they can get is a toothless old man (he does have dentures) who tamed horses in his youth. His name is Francisco Nicomedes Rojas and he's from a small town on the pampas. The lions roar as if they were wild, the old man cracks his whip—you have to admit he looks like he's in danger—but even then the audience isn't happy. They'd do much better with a young woman—blonde, timid looking—but those are too expensive, the lions are saving up.

Lions and Clowns

When the lions eat a clown it's a tragedy. You have to investigate to see if it was an accident, a crime, or a suicide.

When the clowns eat a lion it's a warning. It's important, maybe even urgent, to raise wages.

Three-headed Dog

An enormous dog with three heads and a serpent's tail delights the audience with never-before-seen acts. "Where did they get it?" asks a child. "It's a man in disguise," his mother assures him. "Or perhaps two men."

The dog walks on its hind legs, dances to the beat of the orchestra, smokes cigars, and can guess the name and birthday of all the audience members. It also guesses or knows the dates of their deaths, but doesn't mention them.

The audience has fun. Only a few remember, with confusion, the difficulty of the path. That swollen stream they had to cross to arrive at the circus, that mute and gloomy old man who steered the raft and only accepted coins as payment. What was the name of the river? Why are they so far away from the circus?

They'll all know after the show ends, when they try to exit the big top and find the same dog in their path, silent and fierce, showing the teeth from its three sets of jaws. Only then will they see, on the three heads of Cerberus, the fatal glare of those six cruel and bloodshot eyes.

Horses

No. I'll tell you again that as far as horses go it's all been done. Yes, even that. We've even got Pegasus and I'll guarantee you it's not easy to pay what it costs to take care of him. Don't even talk to me about centaurs—they're brutal, disgusting, and they don't respect the audience. No, I'm sorry, not even that ability impresses me, I've even worked with several descendants of Mr. Ed—yes, that Mr. Ed, the talking horse. It didn't work out, because they were already out of style and, besides, and don't take this personally, what they have to say isn't that interesting. Look, if you want to be famous, you need to realize that no one ever remembers a circus horse's name. I'd encourage you to go back to your stable with your trainer and keep working out for the Derby.

Tiny-animal Tamer

The death of the famous chimpanzee Turk, caused by indigestion from all the sweets given him by women and children, nearly bankrupted his owner. Desperate, the man swore his children would only train much smaller animals, ones much easier to replace. In the 19th century, those animals were unknown to humans, but it didn't take long to discover them.

Today, in the microbe circus, amoebas and paramecia are like elephants. They're docile and stick out for their large size. Spirochetes and Koch's bacillae are the most common and terrifying wild animals: no precaution is too great to protect the audience. Shows take place in laboratories or people's houses. Bigger showings have been tried, with large screens that reproduce the figures on the slides, but this has proved difficult.

The Kiss of Death

There's the act, common worldwide, where a person puts his or her head in a lion's mouth. In circuses in India they call it "the kiss of death," and it's not performed by the tamer but by one of his assistants. Some years ago, after a long strike, the assistants gained the right to put on a motorcycle helmet before starting. For its part, the lions' union now demands the presence of a dentist just outside the cage.

Clowns and Animals

In former times, a lot of clowns performed with animals. The English clown Dicky Usher sailed the Thames in a barrel pulled by eight swans. When he arrived at Waterloo Bridge, he got into a cart pulled by eight cats to go to the theatre where he was performing.

In Russia, the Duroff brothers had a pig named Chuska that they would push from a blimp in a parachute. One day the parachute didn't open up in time. According to rumors spread by jealous competitors, Chuska must have demanded too big a raise.

Circus History

I Am

I am the metal beams that hold up the big top and the nylon fabric from which it is made, I am the lion and the tiger and the liger and the bear, I am the covered wagon and the lights and the sequins on the equestrienne's suit, I am the trapeze and the trapeze artist and the rope up which the acrobats climb, I am the darkness above the abyss, I am chaos, I am the word that divided light from darkness, I am He who said let there be circus and the circus rose up out of the waters and it was good.

Others say the modern circus was born at the end of the 18th century, when Philip Astley, a sergeant in the British army, discovered that, thanks to centrifugal force, a man could stand up on a horse that was galloping in circles.

Both versions are plausible and can be simultaneously true.

Naumachias and Pantomimes

In the beginning they imitated us. The ancient Romans, more than anyone, achieved a level of perfection. In the circus pantomimes, the actors were typically criminals condemned to death. They would enter the arena with gold-embroidered tunics and purple capes. The clothing was shortly lit on fire and the wrongdoers would burn to death. The public called these garments the *tunica molesta*, the uncomfortable tunic. These would also be smeared with resin: The blaze would convert the people into human torches that would light up the night. Sometimes the pantomimes would recreate historic events or tragic myths, like the castration of Attis.

But the pitched battles and most of all the naumachias, the simulated naval battles, were much bloodier due to the number of participants. The most significant naumachia was the one organized by the emperor Claudius in the year 52 A.D. In an enormous artificial lake where a simulated Sicilian fleet battled a simulated Rhodian fleet, 19,000 men fought to the death.

Among us, no show has been as successful as that of World War II, for its duration and for the number of people involved. Nevertheless, when it ended, some people condemned it: Fifty-five million people had died, and that's not easy to top. From that point on, and especially since the development of nuclear weapons (how wonderfully inventive they are!), we prefer limited confrontations, like Vietnam, tribal wars in Africa, the war on terror, the Balkans, situations that ultimately have limits and allow us to enjoy the show and make bets without truly risking the complete destruction of this entertaining and warlike species.

Theory of the Hundred Exercises

The golden age of Chinese acrobatics occurred between the Han and Song Dynasties, its end coming at the hands of barbarians in the year 1126 C.E. During the Han Dynasty, the emperor Yang Han made an inventory of all the acrobatic disciplines practiced at the time called the Theory of the Hundred Exercises, or Baixi. According to the emperor's enemies, when the book was finished, Yang Han demanded that every acrobat capable of performing acts not found in his book be brought to him. When the emperor personally verified the absolute originality of their acts, each artist was rewarded with 100 ingots of gold and then beheaded.

Juan Moreira

Toward the end of the 19th century, a novel with the title *Juan Moreira* was published in Argentina. It told of the fortunes and misfortunes of a rebellious gaucho. It was so successful that the sad end of the gaucho Juan Moreira became a circus act, with emphasis on the handling of the fighting knives. It's said that from time to time in some lost pueblo, a naïve spectator, confused by how real the show seemed, would jump into the ring with his knife, ready to defend Moreira in his battle against authority.

This spontaneous intervention would typically have a great effect on the rest of the audience, which would applaud, laugh, stomp, and cheer for the spectacle. It got to the point that the director decided to incorporate it into the show. To make the trick work, they would plant someone in the audience who was locally known. Thus, in each small town, they would hire some bum, the type who could be seen drinking gin at all hours of the day, to act as the naïve spectator.

It so happened that in one town they unwittingly came across an ex-police chief who had been relieved of his position for drinking too much. The man, hooked by the chance he was being given, pretended to accept the role in order to obtain his life's dream: to catch the famous Juan Moreira. During the show, very drunk, he leapt into the ring as if to defend him, pulled out a gun, and blew away the actor playing the gaucho. Judged and condemned, he never did understand what he was being punished for.

Ammunition

The creator of the trick or discipline of the human cannonball was an Italian soldier named Farini. In reality, human cannonballs are not expelled by an explosion of gunpowder, but by a hydraulic or compressed-air mechanism. (Gunpowder is used in the circus for its auditory, olfactory, and visual effects.) The first human cannonball was a 14-year-old girl, shot out in 1877.

Unlike ordinary cannonballs, human cannonballs can be used over and over again. For this reason, though they require some maintenance, their use is recommended as ammunition in many manuals of galactic warfare.

Illusionists and Jugglers

De Blas and Matheu note that in the ancient Orient, approximately 3,000 years ago, jugglers and acrobats were already traveling together in troupes, using all kinds of objects like weapons (common martial arts instruments), children's toys (diabolos and devil sticks), and cooking utensils (porcelain jars) that they would toss and catch with different parts of their bodies. The famous juggler Tse Ling Puan of the court of Emperor Chaung was capable of keeping up to five castles in the air at the same time. Some consider him the inventor of illusionism.

The First Fire Eater

Eunus was a Syrian and a slave, ingenious and rebellious. In the year 133 B.C. he became (though he never knew it) the first bona fide fire eater in the Western World. He was the leader of a slave revolt in Sicily where he took several cities and even crowned himself king. As proof of the divine destiny guiding him, he led his desperate troops spitting fire, smoke, and sparks. He held in his mouth a nutshell filled with fiery material, embers and sulfur, breathing through its perforations, like a bellows over hot coals. In the Cirque du Soleil he would have been a great artist. When he was taken alive, the Roman mob merely quartered him, in a show that was undoubtedly interesting but impossible to repeat.

Caligula, Criminals, and Wild Animals

It's not true that Caligula sent criminals to fight against the wild animals of the circus. It was tried, but the criminals were neither showmen nor artists, they weren't conscious of the demands of the audience, they killed the beasts for the sake of killing, to save their own lives, or they were eaten without style or effort. What Caligula did do was order that the wild animals be fed with the flesh of criminals, which is a very different thing.

Unanticipated Laughter

Pepino 88, a clown famous throughout Argentina, wasn't English. His name was José Podestá. The Englishman was Frank Brown, whom Argentinean children called "Fran Bron." Both performed in Buenos Aires at the end of the 19ᵗʰ century. There was another clown, less known but still successful, who didn't have a name or else never told it. His specialty was making children and adults laugh in uncomfortable situations like wakes, school exams, hospital visits, or corporate meetings. Many say he's still out there, practicing his secret art and trying, without success, to get some circus to give him a job: The directors are afraid his presence will ruin the risky acts or at least make them more difficult.

Buffalo Bill

William F. Cody, also known as Buffalo Bill, defended and fed many caravans crossing the American west, killing Indians and buffalos. Through the speed and sureness of his shooting, he became a living legend. But he had been born too late, right at the end of the epic of the West, which ended, for him, before its time: there weren't enough buffalos left, enough Indians.

In the last years of his life, Buffalo Bill organized and ran his own circus: the gigantic Wild West Show, where he exhibited his shooting skill, some giant buffalos, and many of the Indians he had fought against. He was happier than most people imagine.

When a reporter once interviewed him after a show, Buffalo Bill confessed that there was an activity where he was as fast as when he was shooting, but what a shame, it wasn't something that could be shown in public. With a playful, conspiratorial smile, promising he wouldn't publish it or tell anyone, the reporter invited him to open up off the record. I am, said Buffalo Bill with a melancholy sigh, a good reader.

The Whipping Acrobat

A fundamental part of an English prince's education was the whipping boy. When the prince did something wrong, the whipping boy was given the punishment that was forbidden to execute on His Majesty's sacred being.

The famous Italian acrobat Archange Tuccaro, author of the first treatise on leapers and flyers (*Trois Dialogues*, Paris, 1599) was hired to teach acrobatics to the emperor Maximilian of Austria. According to the testimony of an eyewitness, whenever the monarch made a clumsy move while doing a somersault through the air, a young tumbler fell to the ground in his place. As Maximilian had very little talent for this type of activity, the young acrobats, with their broken bones, had to be replaced frequently.

The Feat of Philippe Petit

In 1974, the French tightrope walker Philippe Petit crossed eight times between the twin towers of the World Trade Center walking on a wire.

His feat was less impressive to us than to the inhabitants of this planet, which we arrived at from a distant star by walking carefully, one appendage in front of the other, on that thread strung between the Petronas Towers in Malaysia and our own pointy Kalñs in the Orion system.

It was hard work, but the applause from our spectators made it worthwhile. Or rather, you might call it applause, or, well, I've never managed to understand the subtleties, the complex associations of earthly languages. You could call it applause or, perhaps, tsunami, tidal wave.

Untamable

The idea of an elephant walking on a tightrope is an obvious possibility for fiction. In reality, however, there was just one animal tamer in the whole history of the circus who achieved it. It was Dan Rice (1823-1900), the famous American clown who was a good friend of President Lincoln and himself a candidate for the presidency of the United States. His amazing ability as a tamer allowed him to star in extraordinary acts: in one of them there was a hog named Sybil that was capable of telling time with a certain precision; in another, there was a trained rhinoceros. It's said, however, that he never got his wife to serve him a nice warm supper. She would apparently just tell him what time it was, but she didn't do it as well as Sybil.

Gaetulians and Pachyderms I

They tell of the Numidians of the North, the Gaetulians of the plateaus, and the Garamantes of the desert who inhabited the Sahara. They tell of the Gaetulians, experts with javelins, joining the Roman armies as ancillary troops, unlike the Garamantes. They tell of the Gaetulians caring for the elephants on the voyage across the sea which would finally take them to Rome and its circus, where they would be obligated to kill them for the pleasure and diversion of nearly the whole populace and some poets, like Statius and Martial. They tell of the crossing being long and hard: the Gaetulians and pachyderms, hardly used to traveling in boats, got seasick. They tell the wrenching story of a Gaetulian who fell in love with his elephantess and chose to drive his javelin into his own heart rather than murder his beloved, moving the masses to spare her life. They tell of the birth, almost two years later, of an elephant who was somewhat stupid but nevertheless learned in just a few months how to handle a javelin with his trunk. They tell a lot of wild stories in Rome, just like everywhere else, that are hard or impossible to prove.

Gaetulians and Pachyderms II

The victory over the Carthaginians assures Rome of a supply of exotic animals from North Africa for use in its circus games. Bloody public battles are organized in the arena, risky but not necessarily fatal for the men who get involved. During his second consulship, Pompey offers the first elephant battle. The iron barriers protecting the spectators barely withstand the furious charge of the beasts fighting to escape. They're being chased by Gaetulians with javelins.

After their failed escape attempt, the animals gather in the center of the arena and trumpet their death song. The spectators, perhaps more frightened than moved, call down curses on Pompey, according to Pliny in his Natural History.

Since human beings aren't aware of the existence of parallel universes, Pliny is ignorant of the fact that, simultaneously, the Gaetulians are crushed by the pachyderms, who topple the barriers and savagely take over the streets of Rome and that, for that reason, we pachyderms are here telling this story and somewhere else it's the Gaetulians and somewhere else it's the javelins.

Robert Houdin and the Steel Box

If his disciple Houdini was more than anything an athlete, the key to Robert Houdin's tricks was his profession as a watchmaker. Nevertheless, the most important thing for both of them, as for all illusionists, was their psychological understanding of the illusion, their acute perception of where to apply their deception.

One of Houdin's tricks consisted of showing a light steel box, one even a child could lift, and afterwards asking the strongest men in the audience to move it while an enormous magnet in the floor kept it in place. The trick was a great success when Houdin claimed that his magical power consisted of increasing the weight of the box. But he soon discovered that the people were much more impressed if he claimed to be capable of stealing a man's strength, making him so weak that he could no longer move the box—just like some authors who, instead of recognizing their novel's actual weight, blame the weakness of the reader. This trick can be done without magnets, but it's necessary to count on the steely support of the critics.

Variety Shows

When variety shows were popular in Germany, they threatened the very existence of the circus there. Lured by the good contracts and the possibility of acting in smaller spaces that made for a better rapport with the audience, many performers left the circus for the music hall. Illusionists particularly benefited from working in a theater that allowed them to stand before an audience whose field of view never exceeded 180 degrees as opposed to the 360 degrees of attentive eyes at the circus ring. The Great Corbelli (or Bertold Luftmensch) was the only artist to multiply his salary by acting in a circus and a variety show on the same day at the same time but, as he was not an illusionist but a magician, he transformed himself in such a way that no one noticed. Some even say there were two of him.

Ethnic Troupes

It was Louis Dejean, the friendly director of the French circus, who was the first to show ethnic troupes composed of lesser-known ethnicities. Authentic Nubians, Hottentots, Inuits (then called Eskimos), and Sioux passed through the 19th century in the circus rings and vaudevilles of Europe. One of these troupes, native to the sunken continent of Atlantis, delighted the audience for a single magical night, before going extinct because of the choreographer, who had the terrible idea of having them take a bow out of the water.

Fantasies

I agree with you, but no, your show won't work for me . . . . You're right about that, otherwise the TV shows that depict disasters wouldn't be successful. Natural ones or personal ones, of course. I'm sorry, but that's not the point. On the contrary, this type of show originated in the circus. Yes, besides those you mention, I could mention others from the 19ᵗʰ century, like "The Taking of the Bastille" or "The Battle of Waterloo," and that's just talking about Astley. Sure, I also remember that one, it was very famous, "The San Francisco Earthquake"; it was shown at the beginning of the 20ᵗʰ century. No, I'll say it again, I'm absolutely sure that "The Hiroshima Bomb" would not be a success, not even with the presence or representation of the cancer-stricken children. Now "The Twin Towers," that one would be possible, but not in this part of the world, of course.

A Bearded Woman

Some stories don't even give your imagination a chance.

On a trip through Mexico in 1854, a circus promoter noticed the servant girl of one of his hosts. She was a shockingly hairy girl of twenty or so years. She looked like a bearded orangutan. She had protruding jaws, a double row of teeth (like a dogfish), a slim waist, and natural feminine grace. We don't know if she followed him for love, money, or adventure, or to escape the tragic tedium of her life. The promoter exhibited Julia Pastrana all over the world; he made her famous and possibly happy.

She was already a pro when Theodore Lent met her. To swipe her from her agent, he married her. That way, in addition to getting what she made at the circus, he could sell much more expensive tickets to their own house, where the monkey woman would serve tea to the fascinated guests. Lent got his wife pregnant and sold tickets to the birth, which took place in Moscow in 1860. The baby was born with the same characteristics as its mother and died two days later. Julia died three days later, always surrounded by spectators. Lent had the corpses embalmed and sold them to the University of Moscow. Nevertheless, when he learned that the university was exhibiting the mummies for "scientific" reasons, he reclaimed the bodies of his wife and child and took them with him to exhibit throughout the world. Some time later on, in Sweden, Theodore Lent married another bearded woman. He died insane in 1880.

Some stories don't even give your imagination a chance.

Illusions

In the 19th century, Napoleon III's Second French Empire sent the famous illusionist Robert Houdin to Algeria to quell an Arab rebellion. Houdin's mission was to use his tricks to outdo the false miracles of the religious leaders who sustained the rebels. It worked—the skilled illusionist managed to overcome and discredit the mullahs, diminishing their influence. In 1962, Algeria gained its independence, ripping the French authorities from their own world of illusions.

War and Acrobatics

In China it's said that during the time of the Yellow Emperor, various generals deserted the imperial army and used their martial arts skills to develop Chinese acrobatics, becoming traveling performers.

Capoeira was a fighting technique created and developed by black slaves in Brazil. With time it became an acrobatic dance, almost a circus art.

Chief Black Eagle and his troupe of Sioux Indians, capable of shooting arrows at a full gallop, traveled Europe with the German Sarrasani circus at the beginning of the 20th century with the approval of the United States government.

The bow shooting of the Central African Pygmies, the pole skills of some indigenous peoples of Tanzania, and the Watusi javelin-thrower acts that are enjoyed nowadays in African circuses—all of these were originally arts of death, of war.

Remembering the lessons of history, we humans who have managed to survive are now preparing games with machine guns, coordinated tank dances, miniature nuclear explosions. When the war is lost, there's always the circus.

Anniversary Celebration

The poet Calpurnius describes one of Nero's celebrations in which the circus floor opened up and from the cellars below there arose a complete forest, with real but gilded trees, fragrant fountains, and wild animals imported from Africa.

In the games offered to the Roman people by Septimius Severus in 202 A.D., the arena was suddenly transformed into an enormous boat, which promptly came undone and released 700 wild animals onto the sand including lions, panthers, bears, buffalos, and ostriches.

Much later, in the festivals organized by the Emperor Pletoricus to celebrate the 10,000th anniversary of the founding of Rome, there appeared before the marveling gaze of the spectators an authentic and ancient space ship from the 26th century. As the hatch opened, a group of humans got out of the ship. The wonder and delight of the audience were boundless, since the majority of those present didn't know that there still existed members of that species, who then died fighting bravely in the midst of a historic ovation.

Ana María Shua is one of contemporary Latin America's most exciting and prolific writers. She was born in Buenos Aires in 1951 and published her first book at age 16. Since then, she has published over 80 books in a multitude of genres and has won numerous national and international awards, including a Guggenheim fellowship. Shua writes in the tradition of Borges, Cortázar, and Denevi, playing with language and our sense of reality. Her books and short stories have been translated into many languages and published worldwide, and her book *Laurita's Loves* was made into a movie. She currently lives in Buenos Aires with her husband, photographer Silvio Fabrykant.

Steven J. Stewart was awarded a 2005 Literature Fellowship for translation by the National Endowment for the Arts. His book of translations of Spanish poet Rafael Pérez Estrada, *Devoured by the Moon* (Hanging Loose Press, 2004) was a finalist for the 2005 PEN-USA translation award. His book of the selected microfictions of Ana María Shua was published in 2009 by the University of Nebraska Press. He presently lives in Rexburg, Idaho.